msc 4/97

CRY
OF THE
BENU BIRD

AN EGYPTIAN CREATION STORY

Adapted and Illustrated by C. Shana Greger

Houghton Mifflin Company · Boston · New York · 1996

For information about this and other Houghton Mifflin
trade and reference books and multimedia products,
visit The Bookstore at Houghton Mifflin on the World Wide
Web at (http://www.hmco.com/trade/).

Library of Congress Cataloging-in-Publication Data

Greger, C. Shana (Carol Shana)
    Cry of the benu bird: an Egyptian creation story / C. Shana Greger.
        p.   cm.
    Summary: Tells how Nun, "a sleeping ocean of deep water surrounded
on all sides by Chaos," brings forth first Benu, a magnificent
glowing bird, and then Atum, Shu, Tefnut, and the rest of creation.
    ISBN 0-395-73573-4
    [1. Creation—Folklore.   2. Folklore—Egypt.]   I. Title.
PZ8.1.G864Cr   1996   [398.2'0962]—dc20
95-16358   CIP   AC

Manufactured in Singapore

TWP   10   9   8   7   6   5   4   3   2   1

For Betty and Bill

Author's Note

There are three separate groups of Egyptian myths, each named for an ancient city: Heliopolis, Hermopolis, and Memphis. The myths can be confusing; even stories from the same group are inconsistent. In writing *Cry of the Benu Bird,* I combined several different Heliopolitan legends. Accounts of the original myths I referred to can be found in *The Egyptian Book of the Dead, The Ancient Egyptian Coffin Texts,* and *The Pyramid Texts.*

I used much of the basic Heliopolitan creation story: Atum (pronounced "ah-tum") creates Shu (pronounced like "shoe") and Tefnut ("nut" rhymes with "boot"), who in turn produce two children, Geb (pronounced like "get") and Nut (pronounced like "newt"). Nut's children are the sun, moon, and planets. In Egyptian belief, Atum is worshiped as three different forms of the sun, and I adapted accounts of Re-Atum ("re" is pronounced like "ray"), the noonday sun, for Atum's birth and for the creation of the minor gods, humans, and animals.

For ancient Egyptians, the Benu Bird was not only a symbol of eternity but also a protector against darkness. It was believed that the sun rose in the form of the Benu Bird, and that the bird was actually the soul of the sun-god Re. The story of the Benu Bird's regeneration came from the legend as told by Herodotus, a fifth-century Greek historian.

In *Cry of the Benu Bird,* I combined the stories of the Benu Bird and Atum through their shared relationship to the sun. The idea that the light of the Benu Bird exists within Atum and all that he created is my own.

The Beginning of Time

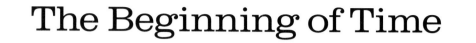

efore the beginning of time there was a sleeping ocean called Nun, surrounded by Chaos. In the darkness, Chaos swirled furiously against Nun. After uncounted ages, Nun awoke.

A glowing bird burst from Nun's waters, lighting the darkness for the very first time. Afraid of the light, Chaos fled.

Nun spoke. "You are Benu, which means Brilliant Rising." The bird tilted back his head and opened his beak wide.

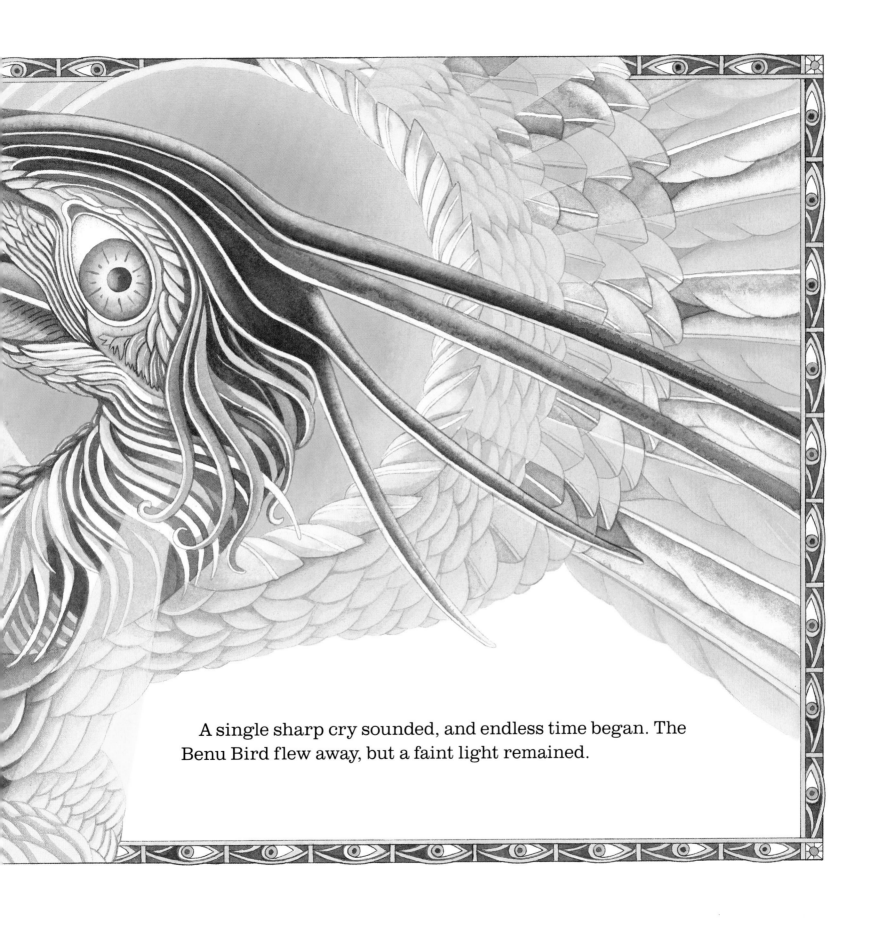

A single sharp cry sounded, and endless time began. The Benu Bird flew away, but a faint light remained.

The Complete One

nce more, Nun stirred. A lotus flower emerged from the waters, and a child rose up in its center. Cradled in Nun, the boy grew. When he was fully grown, Nun spoke. "Your name is Atum, which means Complete One, and you will continue the work of creation." Nun paused, then added, "Beware of Chaos. It seeks to return all to darkness." Then Nun slept.

Atum was lonely. He sighed, and his sigh became a thick fog that separated into air and moisture. The air became a young lion and the moisture a young lioness. Atum tried to catch his children, but they tumbled farther into Nun.

Despairing, Atum cried so hard that one of his eyes loosened, and he sent it to search for his children. The eye roamed through Nun, shining light into every dim place. At last it found them huddled together.

Atum drew near. "Your name is Shu, or Life," he said to his son, "and your name is Tefnut, or Order," he said to his daughter. They all clung together in Nun, and gradually the children changed to their father's form.

Again Nun stirred. "Atum, your children are grown. Kiss Tefnut farewell and let her go with Shu and be married."

As Atum kissed Tefnut, Shu pushed himself up, and a mound of land rose with him. The air grew brighter. Atum looked around in wonder, then turned to his children. "It is time for you to go away together, so that creation may continue." Tefnut and Shu obeyed, and Atum rested on the mound, gazing through the haze at the distant Nun.

Day and Night

As time passed, more land appeared, dotted with lakes and streams, and the mound became a mountain. Shu and Tefnut returned with a son named Geb, or Earth, and a daughter named Nut, or Sky. Together, Atum and his children and grandchildren built a city on the mountain and declared it the center of the world. Then Shu and Tefnut went out as lions to explore the Earth.

In time, Geb and Nut grew up. They worked together, Nut keeping the lakes full while Geb groomed their edges, and at last they married. When their parents returned, Shu was furious. Standing on Geb, Shu hurled Nut aloft and held her there, her hands to the west and her feet to the east. But Nut was already pregnant and soon gave birth.

Sun was the first-born. The air became brighter than ever before as the fiery disk began moving westward across Nut. "Your name is Re," Atum declared.

Next, the Moon, Stars, and Planets were born. They clung to the pale blue dress of their mother and were almost invisible in the bright light of Re. Soon Re reached the western horizon and Nut swallowed him.

So ended the first day.

The air dimmed, and Nut's dress darkened. The Moon, Stars, and Planets danced upon it as Re traveled inside Nut until he reached the East. There Re was reborn, and the second day began.

Atum named the city on the mountain Heliopolis, or City of the Sun, and a temple was built there to honor Re.

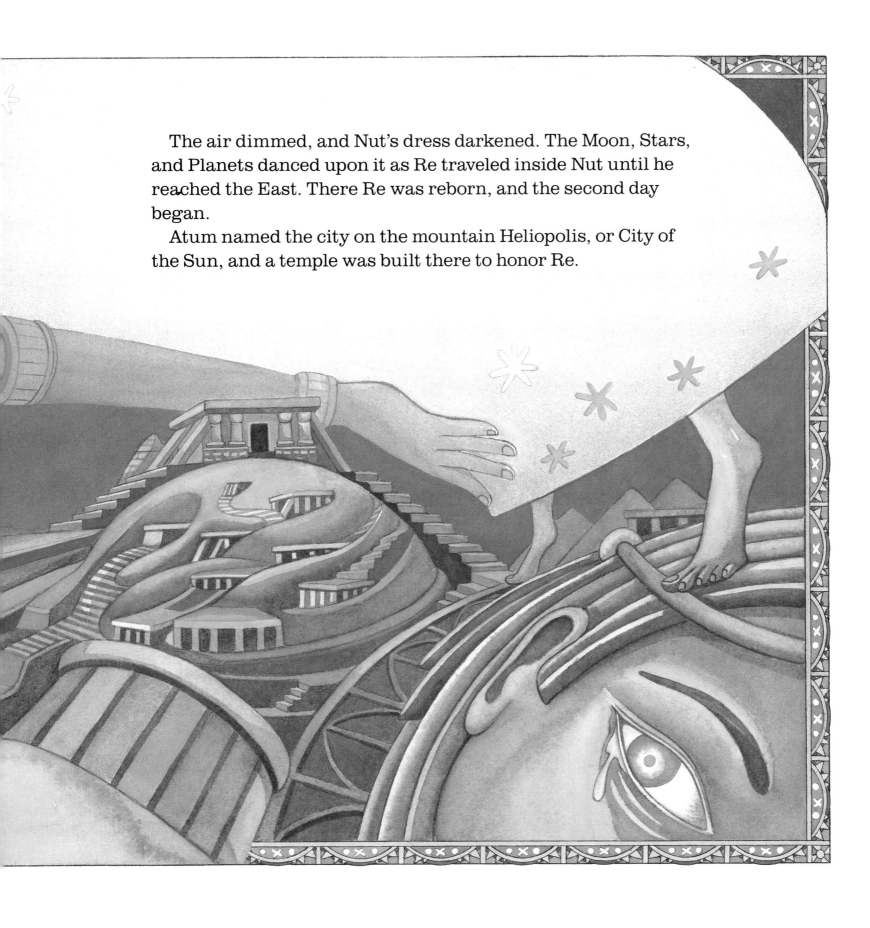

The Rest of Creation

 ife was peaceful in the City of the Sun, but Atum was troubled. He remembered Nun's warning and feared that even Re's light couldn't keep Chaos away.

"I shall create more gods to help," Atum decided. He secluded himself in the temple and strained in thought. Sweat trickled from his body, and each drop became a god or goddess. In this way Atum created hundreds of gods for all purposes.

Atum decided to make creatures to care for the new gods. It saddened him that these beings would not be gods and he wept. As his tears fell, they hardened into human beings.

Finally, Atum called out their names, and every type of animal and plant appeared. In this way Atum created everything on Earth. Afterward, he remained in the Temple of the Sun and watched over his creation.

Return of the Benu Bird

ore than five hundred thousand days and nights had now passed. Atum's bones had turned to silver, his flesh to gold, and his hair to lapis lazuli.

Late one afternoon, Atum saw a strange bird flying toward him. It glowed like the Sun and carried a large bundle made of myrrh. As it neared, Atum called out. "Who are you? I didn't create you."

The bird gazed deeply into Atum's eyes, shining light meeting shining light. "I am the child of the first Benu Bird, who began time and drove back Chaos. My father has died, but I will carry on in his place. I have come to the Temple of the Sun to bury his remains." The young bird dug a hole with his beak and buried his bundle under the temple.

"I don't remember your father either," replied Atum.

The bird raised his head. "My father was present in the dim light when you were created and in the hazy light when you kissed your daughter farewell. He is there in the bright light of Re and in all the life you have created." The Benu Bird extended his wings.

"Will I ever see you again?" Atum asked.

"In a very long time. When all Nut's children return to their places again, I will die and be reborn in my own child. He will bury my remains here and carry on in my place." The Benu Bird turned and soared into the sky, vanishing into the light of Re.

Slowly Re disappeared beyond the western horizon. Atum closed his eyes and imagined the time when he would meet the Benu Bird again. He rested, content.